FOREVER

POST CARD

ONE CENT

USA

19¢

2¢

5¢

8¢

AIRMAIL

USA

55¢

$1.00

29 CENTS

To the real Arfy

All rights reserved. Published in the United States by Random House Children's Books,
a division of Penguin Random House LLC, New York.

Random House and the colophon are registered trademarks of Penguin Random House LLC.

Visit us on the Web! rhcbooks.com

Educators and librarians, for a variety of teaching tools, visit us at RHTeachersLibrarians.com

Library of Congress Cataloging-in-Publication Data
Name: Cummings, Troy, author.
Title: Can I be your dog? / Troy Cummings.
Description: First edition. | New York : Random House, [2018] |
Summary: A dog looking for a home sends letters to prospective owners on Butternut Street, with surprising results. |
Description based on print version record and CIP data provided by publisher; resource not viewed.
Identifiers: LCCN 2015043998 (print) | LCCN 2016020399 (ebook) |
ISBN 978-0-399-55452-0 (hardcover) | ISBN 978-0-399-55453-7 (lib. bdg.) | ISBN 978-0-399-55454-4 (ebook)
Subjects: | CYAC: Dogs—Fiction. | Letters—Fiction.
Classification: LCC PZ7.C91494 (ebook) | LCC PZ7.C91494 Can 2017 (print) |
DDC [E]—dc23

MANUFACTURED IN CHINA

10 9 8 7 6 5 4 3 2 1

First Edition

CAN I BE YOUR DOG?

TROY
CUMMINGS

Random House 🏠 New York

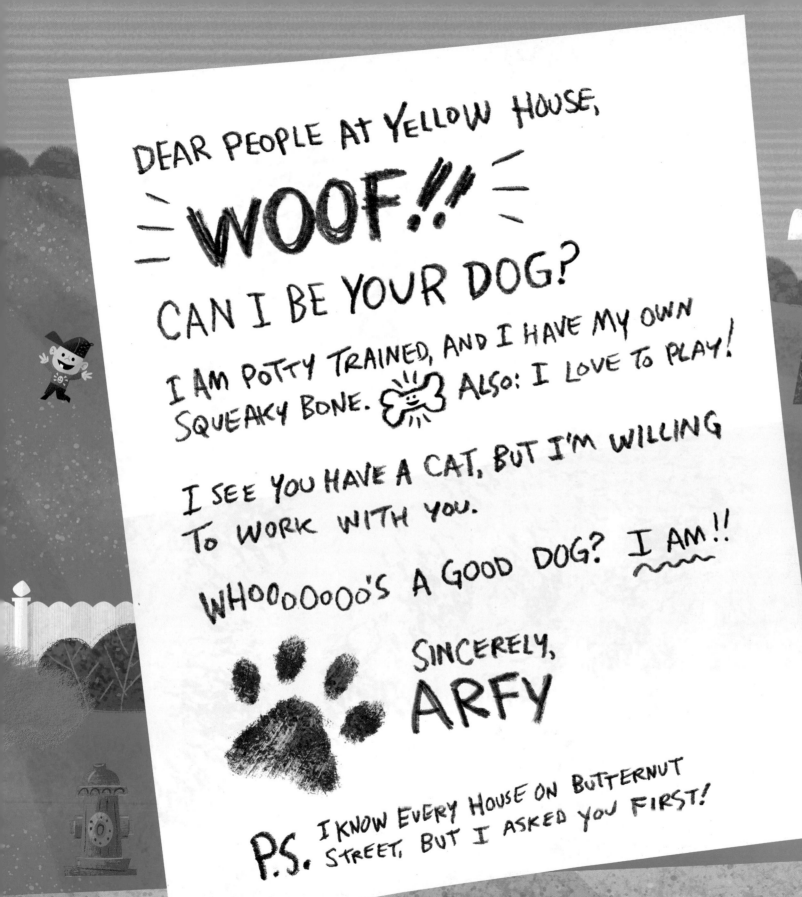

Dear Arfy,

We're so sorry, but you cannot be our dog.
Our cat is, um, allergic to dogs.

Good luck in your search!

The Honeywells

Look, pal.

I've got a bone to pick with you. Last time I let a dog into my shop, a dozen meatballs went missing! Sorry, but there's NO WAY I'm taking in a pooch.

Veronica Shank
BUTCHER

P.S. No hard feelings. Enjoy these dried giblets, and good luck finding a home.

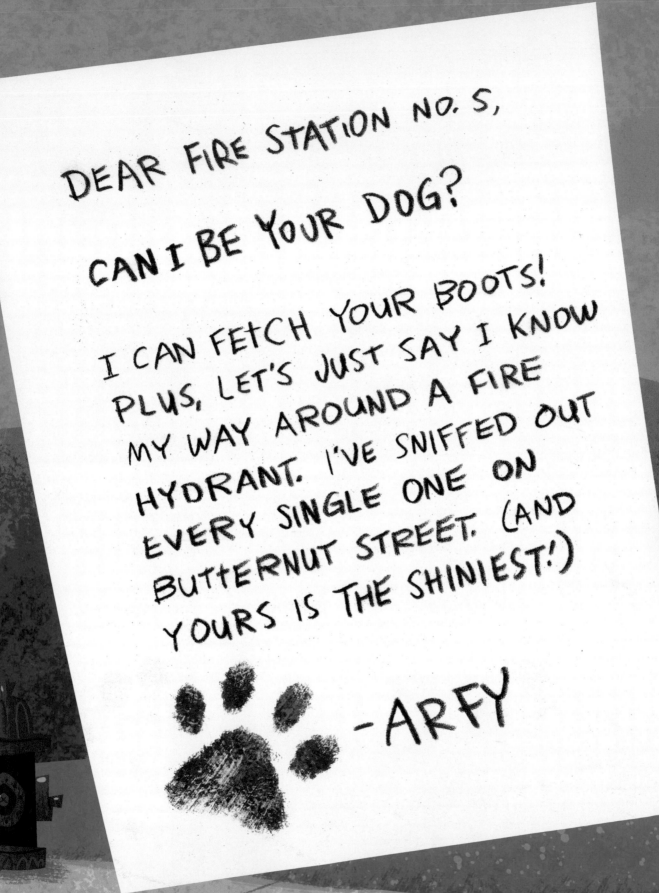

Dear **APPLICANT**:

Thank you for your interest in working with the

BUTTERNUT STREET FIRE STATION.

Unfortunately, the position of:

FIRE DOG

has already been filled.

We will keep your letter on file. Best wishes in your search.

Station No. 5

DEAR LAST HOUSE
ON BUTTERNUT STREET,

CAN I BE YOUR DOG? I SEE THAT
YOUR YARD IS FULL OF WEEDS,
AND YOUR WINDOWS ARE BROKEN.
AND THERE'S A FUNNY SMELL.

BUT I'M NOT PICKY.

JUST LONELY.

-ARFY

Dear Arfy,

Can I be your person?

I need a friend who will be with me no matter what: snow, rain, heat, or gloom of night.

And I see that you already know everyone on Butternut Street!

I know you'll make a first-class partner.

With hugs and head scratches,

Mitzy Whipple
Letter Carrier

P.S. If you agree, meet me at the big blue mailbox.

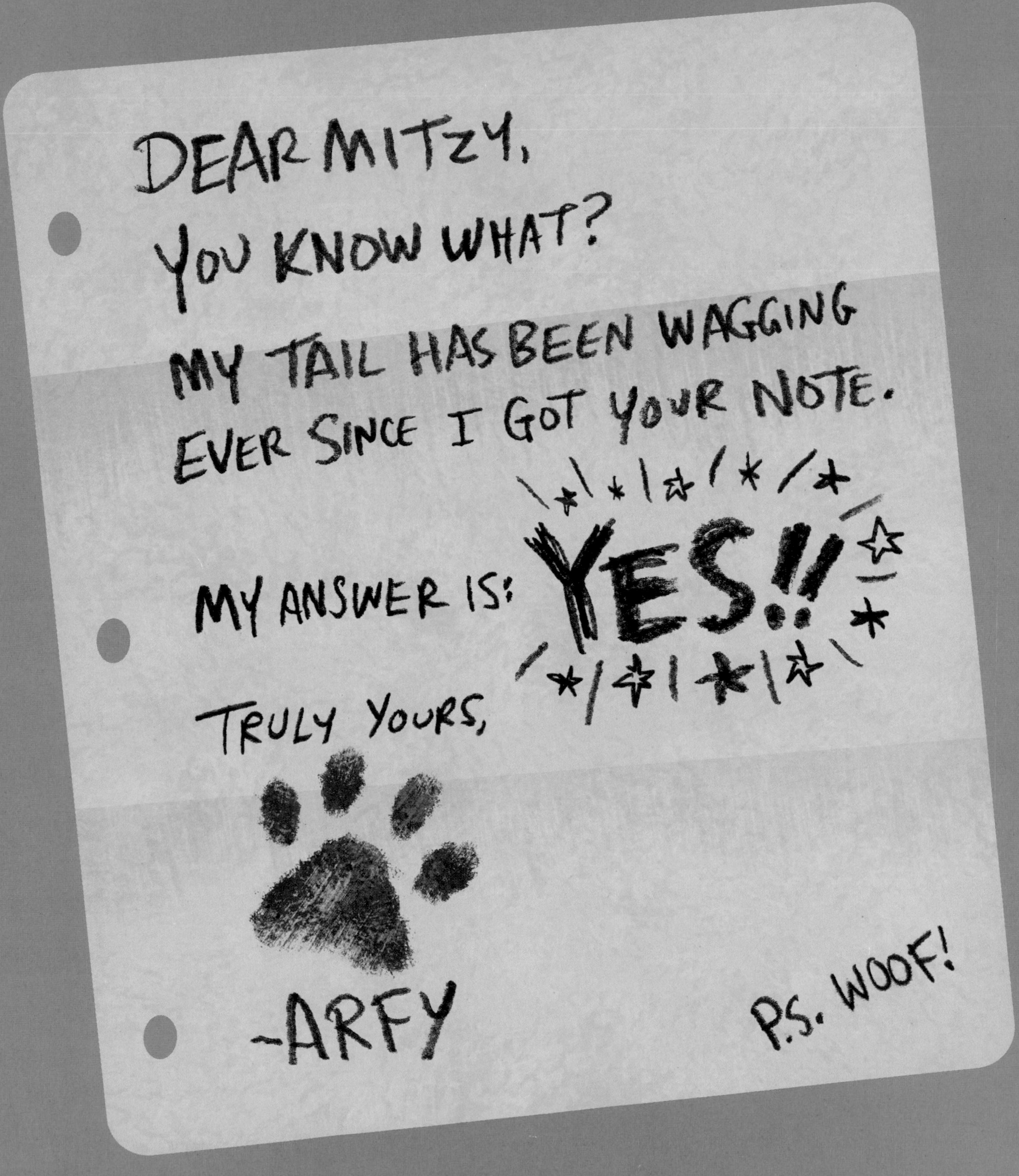
DEAR MITZY,

YOU KNOW WHAT?

MY TAIL HAS BEEN WAGGING
EVER SINCE I GOT YOUR NOTE.

MY ANSWER IS: YES!!

TRULY YOURS,

-ARFY

P.S. WOOF!